P9-DFG-840

the LOST and FOUND

mark teague

SCHOLASTIC PRESS ▾ NEW YORK

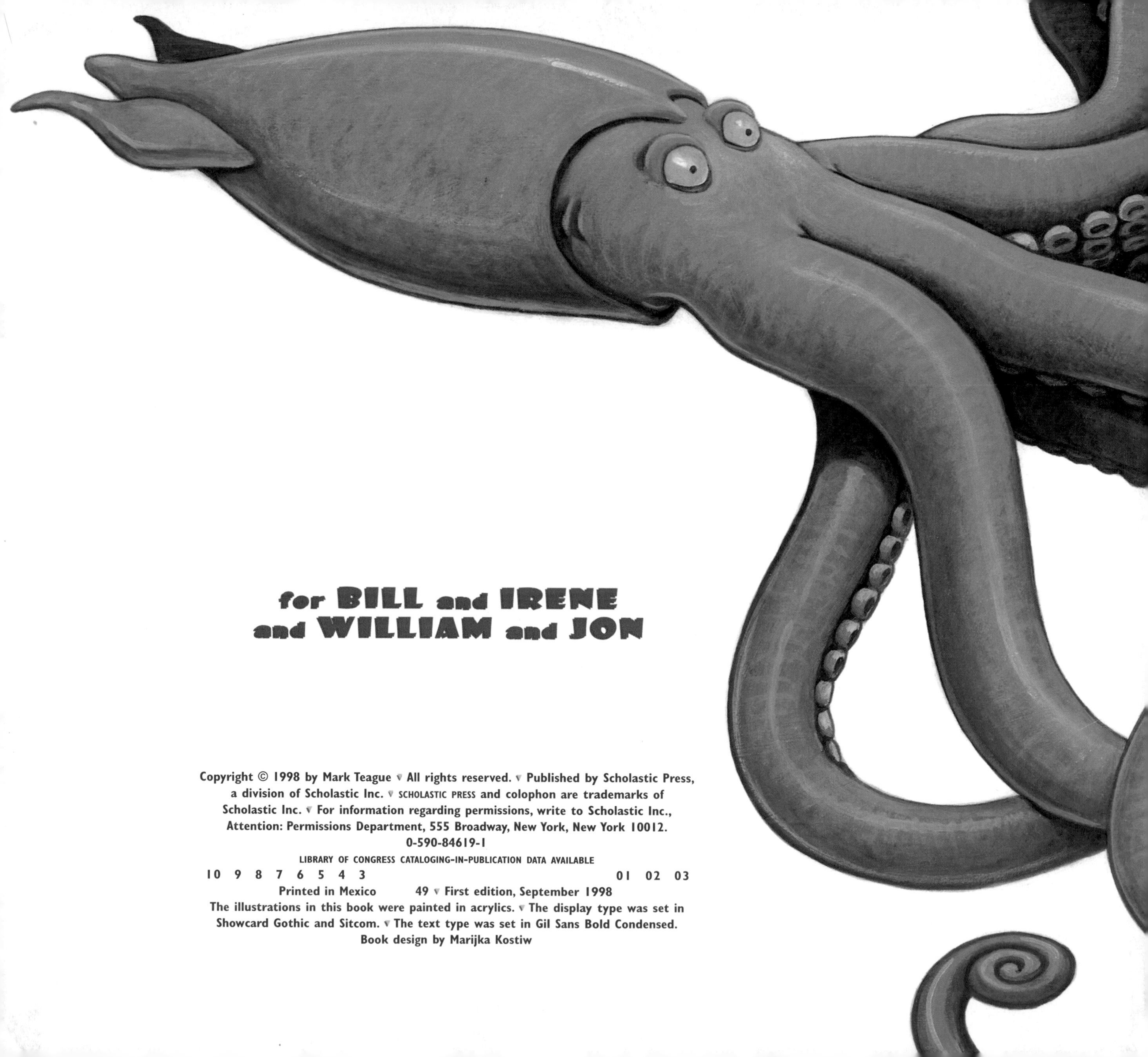

for BILL and IRENE
and WILLIAM and JON

 ▾ Published by Scholastic Press, a division of Scholastic Inc. ▾ SCHOLASTIC PRESS and colophon are trademarks of Scholastic Inc. ▾ For information regarding permissions, write to Scholastic Inc., Attention: Permissions Department, 555 Broadway, New York, New York 10012.
0-590-84619-1
LIBRARY OF CONGRESS CATALOGING-IN-PUBLICATION DATA AVAILABLE
10 9 8 7 6 5 4 3 01 02 03
Printed in Mexico 49 ▾ First edition, September 1998
The illustrations in this book were painted in acrylics. ▾ The display type was set in Showcard Gothic and Sitcom. ▾ The text type was set in Gil Sans Bold Condensed.
Book design by Marijka Kostiw

Wendell and Floyd were in trouble. That morning a giant squid had trapped them in the boys' restroom for almost an hour, causing them to miss a math test. Their teacher, Ms. Gernsblatt, had been furious.

"We have no luck," said Floyd.

Just then, Mona Tudburn entered the office. Mona was the new girl in their class.

"I'm trying to find the Lost and Found," she said. "I lost my lucky hat."

Wendell and Floyd glanced at each other.
"That's strange," said Wendell. "We were just talking about luck."
"We don't have any," Floyd said.
"Neither do I," said Mona. "At least not without my hat."

Wendell pointed to a bin marked LOST AND FOUND. "I wish I had a lucky hat."

"So do I," Floyd agreed. "Then maybe we wouldn't get into these crazy situations."

LOST

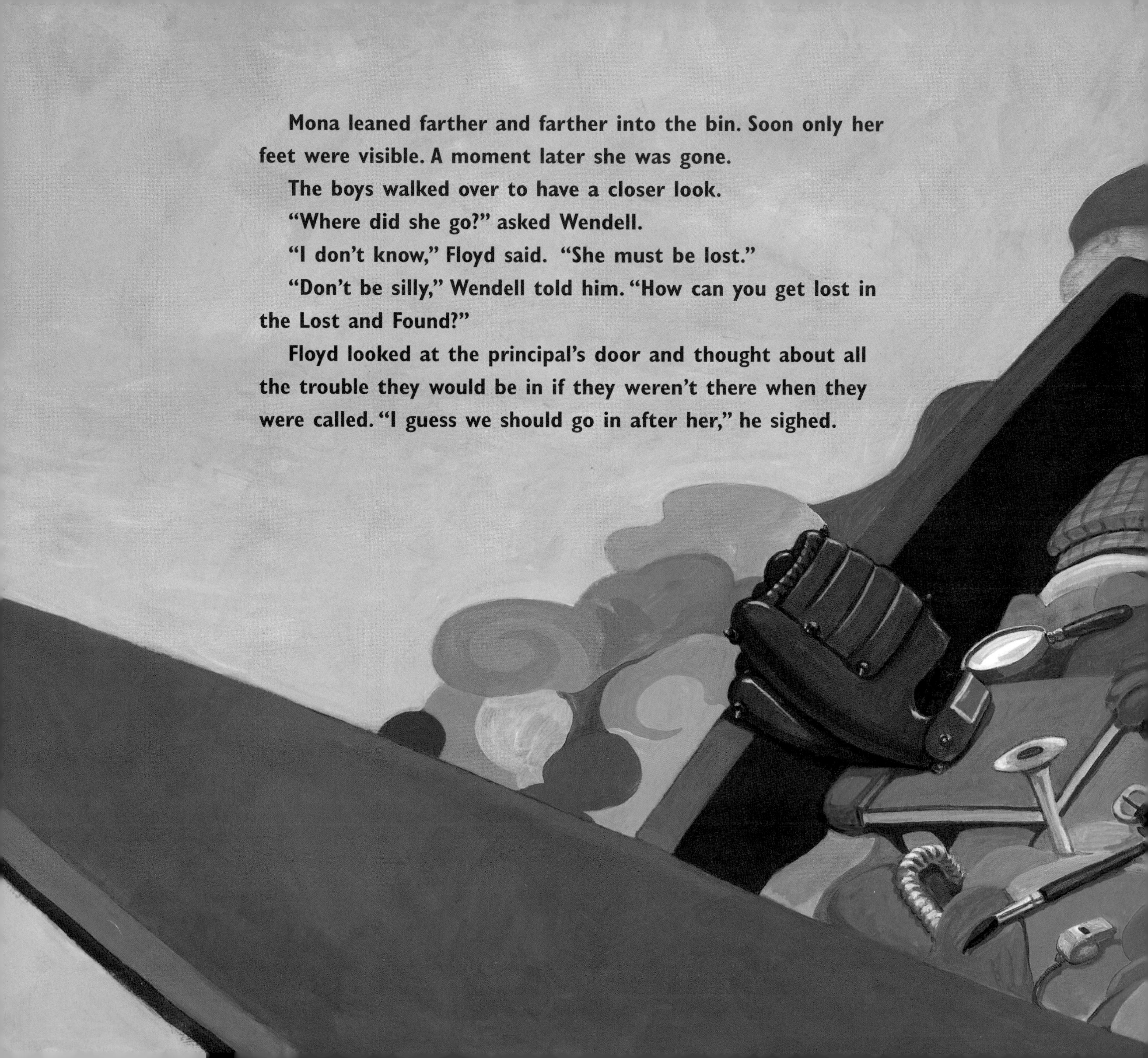

Mona leaned farther and farther into the bin. Soon only her feet were visible. A moment later she was gone.

The boys walked over to have a closer look.

"Where did she go?" asked Wendell.

"I don't know," Floyd said. "She must be lost."

"Don't be silly," Wendell told him. "How can you get lost in the Lost and Found?"

Floyd looked at the principal's door and thought about all the trouble they would be in if they weren't there when they were called. "I guess we should go in after her," he sighed.

They climbed into the bin and instantly plunged into a deep well of lost toys and clothing.

"Look, Floyd, we found Mona."

"I think I found you," Mona said.

"Maybe we should get back now," Floyd suggested.

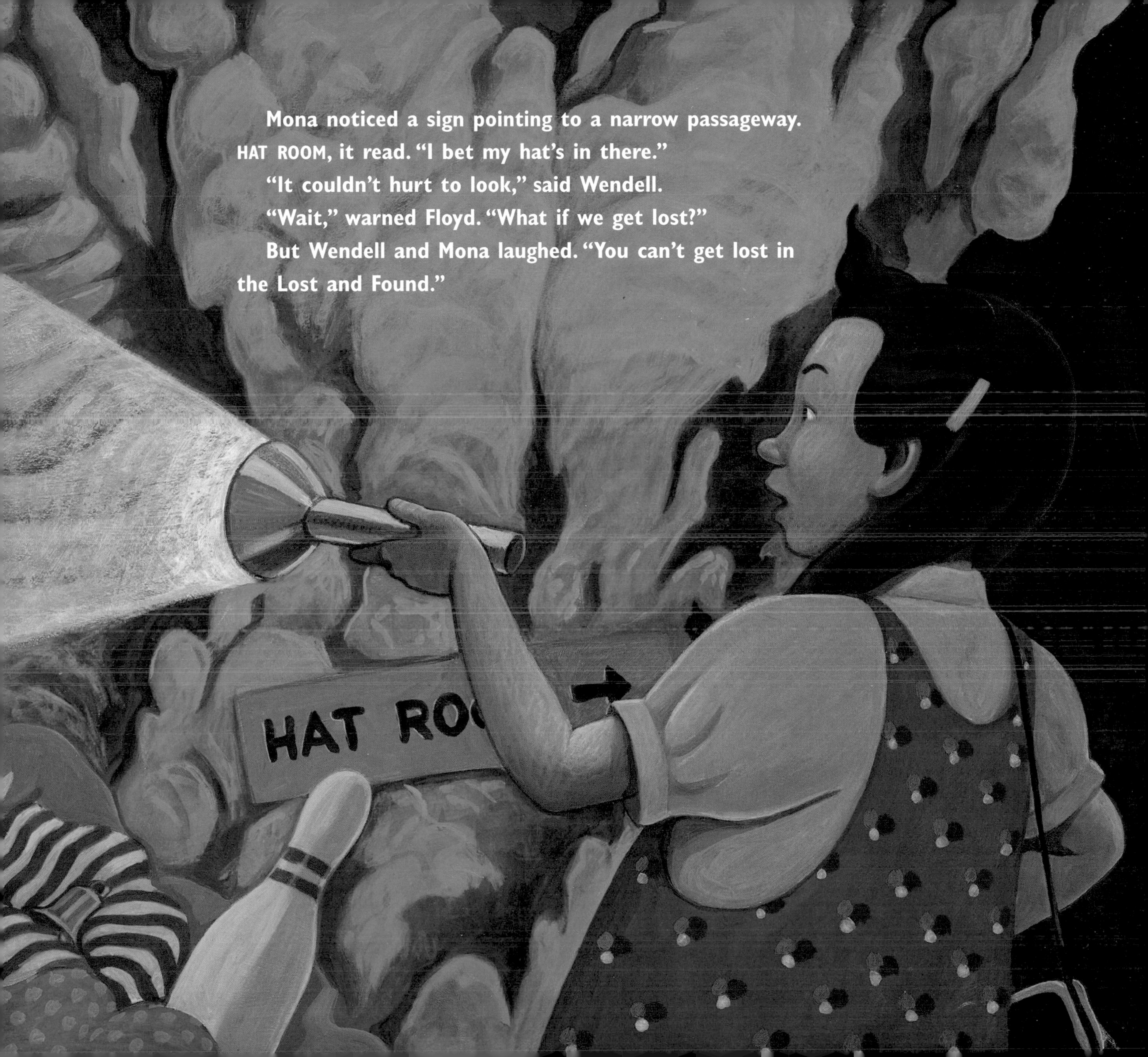

Mona noticed a sign pointing to a narrow passageway. HAT ROOM, it read. "I bet my hat's in there."

"It couldn't hurt to look," said Wendell.

"Wait," warned Floyd. "What if we get lost?"

But Wendell and Mona laughed. "You can't get lost in the Lost and Found."

The passageway led to a cave where a deep lake gurgled and steamed.

"I wonder if the principal knows this is here," said Floyd.

Wendell examined a suit of armor. "Some of this stuff has been lost a long time."

"I still don't see my hat," grumbled Mona.

Then Wendell found a boat. "Perfect! We'll paddle across."

HAT ROOM
ACROSS LAKE →
ATLANTIS →

On the far side of the lake were three tunnels. "Which way do we go now?" asked Floyd.

"We could flip a coin," Wendell suggested.

Mona frowned. "That only works if there are two choices. Here we have three."

The boys thought about that for a while. Finally Wendell threw up his hands, "Let's try the middle one."

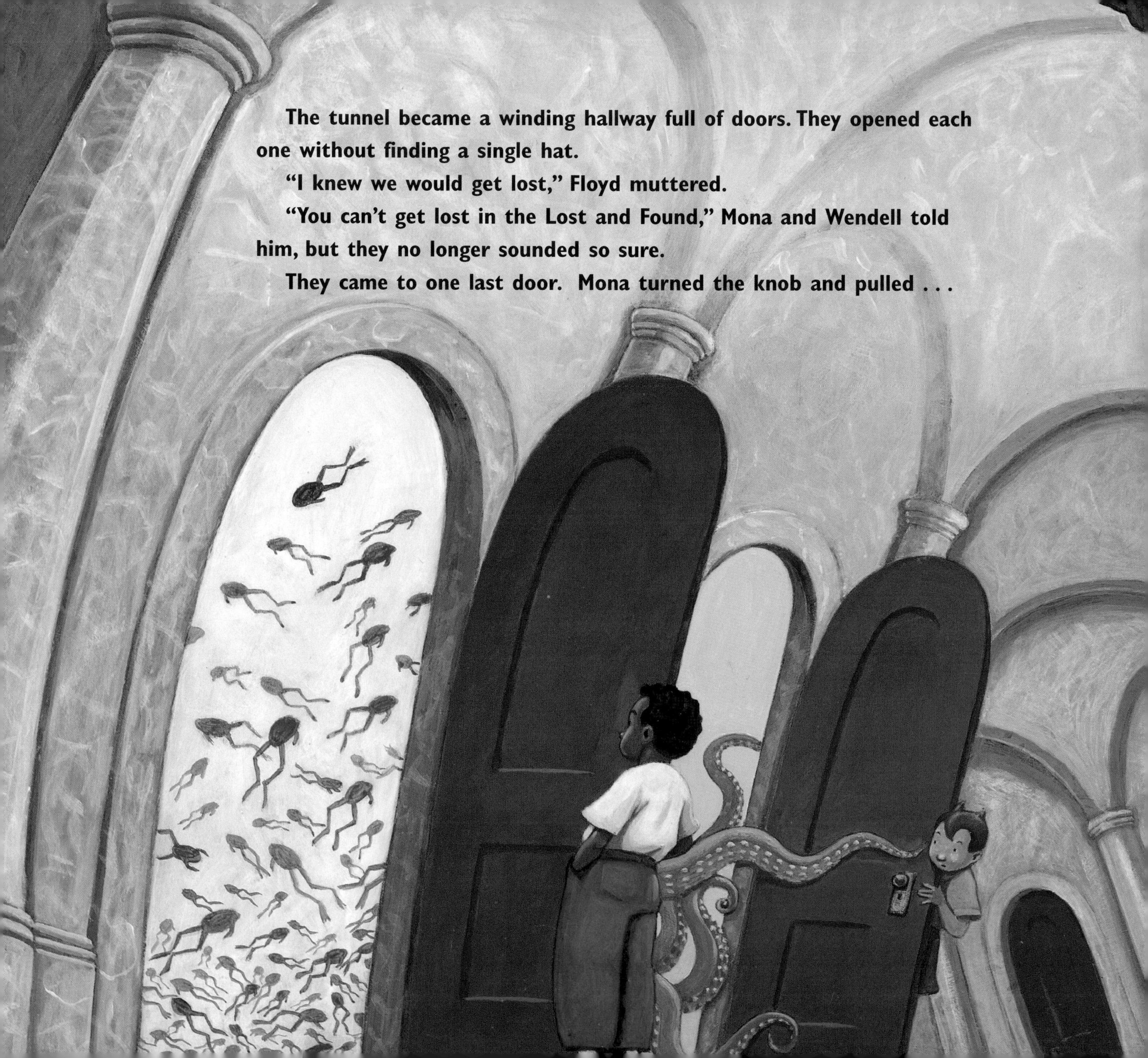

The tunnel became a winding hallway full of doors. They opened each one without finding a single hat.

"I knew we would get lost," Floyd muttered.

"You can't get lost in the Lost and Found," Mona and Wendell told him, but they no longer sounded so sure.

They came to one last door. Mona turned the knob and pulled . . .

“The Hat Room!” cried the boys.

But Mona shook her head in dismay. “There’s too many! I’ll never find my hat in here.”

They decided to look anyway.

"Is it this one?" asked Wendell.

It wasn't.

"How about this one?" Floyd held up a huge pink hat with purple flowers and a canary.

"Of course not," said Mona.

The boys began trying on hats themselves. "How do you tell if one is lucky?" Floyd asked.

"I don't know," said Mona. "It'll just sort of feel lucky."

Wendell tried on a burgundy fez with a small gold tassel. "This one feels lucky."

While Floyd was finding his own lucky hat, Wendell's tassel began to tickle his nose. "I think I'm going to sneeze."

"Hold on. I'll get you a tissue." Mona reached into her purse, and when she did, a strange look came over her face. She held up something green and badly rumpled.

"My lucky hat. I guess it was in my purse all along."

For a moment nobody spoke. Then Floyd sighed, "At least we can go back now."

"Maybe not," Wendell said.

"What do you mean?" asked Floyd and Mona.

"I mean, we might be lost."

Floyd groaned. "I thought you said we couldn't get lost in the Lost and Found."

"It's been an unusual day," said Wendell. "To be honest, I don't even remember which door we came through."

The children looked around. There were doorways in all directions. None of them could remember which one was theirs.

Suddenly Mona laughed. "What are we worried about? We've all got our lucky hats, right?"

She closed her eyes and turned slowly around. When she opened them again, she pointed straight ahead. "I say we go that way."

PRINCIPAL

After a long journey, the children's heads popped out of the Lost and Found bin, just in time to hear the principal call, "Wendell and Floyd, come in here please."

It was late that afternoon before the boys left school. They found their new friend Mona waiting for them.

"How was it?" she asked.

"Not bad," said Floyd.

The principal had merely lectured them about telling the truth. Of course, Ms. Gernsblatt had made them stay and finish their math tests, but it could have been worse.

"I think our luck is changing," said Wendell.

Mona nodded. "Me too."

Since it was late, they decided to take a shortcut.

"I hope we don't get lost," said Floyd, but he wasn't really worried. Neither were Mona and Wendell. They paused for a moment to put on their hats. Then they all started home, feeling lucky together.